To the High Plains Library

Play what's
in your heart!

Inspired by the film

Miguel
and the
Grand
Harmony

Written by Newbery Medal winner
Matt de la Peña

Illustrated by
Ana Ramírez

DISNEP PRESS
Los Angeles • New York

To all the great educators out there who teach young people how to hear the music.

—M. de la P.

In these uncertain times, I would like to dedicate this book to all of you who believe the power of music can break walls, touch hearts, and bring people together.
To Harley Jessup, for giving me a chance.
A mi papá, a mi mami y a mi hermana. Gracias por siempre estar ahí.

—A. R.

Design by Winnie Ho

Printed in the United States of America
First Hardcover Edition, October 2017   10 9 8 7 6 5 4 3 2 1
ISBN 978-1-4847-8149-4
FAC-034274-17237
Library of Congress Control Number: 2017936308
www.disneybooks.com

First comes the sound.
  A single string plucked
or a note blown
    or beat rapped.

And suddenly I am.
Where there is music, there is color.
And where there is color, there is life.

I roam this vibrant city determined to keep the gray at bay.
"La Música," I hear their hearts beckon. "We need you."
To create a grand harmony, I need them, too.

Here I am tucked inside the buzz of wedding bells,
the band shifting into ballad and every hand linked
around the glowing bride and groom.

Here I am at a packed pueblo quinceañera,
swaying along with a staticky song
as a fresh-faced girl lifts a tiara onto her head.

Here I am huddled over an open cemetery plot,
breathing life into the quiet reflections of loved ones
and the weeping beauty of a single violin.

Today I fall upon a trio of músicos tuning their instruments.
They laugh from their bellies and wave to passersby.
They shoo away a stray dog.

A fourth músico steps to a trash bin holding a busted guitar.
"She was good to me," he says.
"Until you sat on her," his friend replies.
More laughter as the man tosses the ruined instrument
and returns to his crate.

He thumbs the nylon strings of a new guitar,
and I ride the rhythms across the plaza.

By sundown the alleyways are packed with people,
and I leap from song to song.
On warm nights like this I am the city and the city is me.
But just as my surge of sound is lifting toward the twilight . . .

an old woman barges out of a shoe shop.

"Stop that music!" she shouts. "You'll upset Mamá Coco!"

A startled guitar player fumbles for his favorite hat.
A trumpeter, hurrying to put away his instrument,
knocks over a box of mismatched nails.

Before I am sucked back into nothingness, I notice a boy.
He holds a broom in one hand, a dustpan in the other.
And while everyone else in the shop is busy waving away los músicos,
the boy's eyes are glued to their guitars.
There's music in his heart.
He turns to look for me,
but I'm already lost into a colorless void.

The following morning
I rise with the crowing roosters
and race from place to place.

But all day my thoughts
keep returning to the boy.

I abandon a flock of songbirds
to follow the thudding paws
of a trotting dog.

Halfway down the alley

I pause to peer inside the window of the shoe shop.

But the boy isn't there.

I sigh and watch his family busily making shoes.

There is a kind of harmony about their rhythmic work.

They are doing what they love.

I'm about to retreat into the whistling wind
when I hear a faint rustling coming from above.
I climb these subtle sounds like a rope up to the roof,
where I discover a secret attic.

Inside, the boy is moving around the antenna of a tiny TV.
I redirect his radio waves
so that an old musical performance comes in clearly.
The boy stares, transfixed.
Then he pops a tape into an old VCR and hits RECORD.

He picks up his broom and holds it like a guitar,
moving his fingers along invisible frets.
When the song ends, and the crowd begins to cheer,
the boy rewinds back to the music.

"Miguel!" a man calls out from below.
"¡Ya vente a comer!"
The boy stops the tape and covers the TV
and hurries out of the attic for dinner.

The following day I trail him into the plaza,
where a band of street musicians is performing.
"Dante, vamos," he calls to his dog,
and the two of them wiggle their way to the front.

This close to the music, the boy's face comes alive.
He belongs to the sound.

But just as I'm about to whisper my name into his ear,
his abuelita appears.

She shoos away the stray and pulls the boy
back through the crowd by his elbow.

"M'ijo, stay away from the mariachis!" she tells him.

"I know, but—"

"Do you want to upset Mamá Coco?"

He shakes his head and follows her back to their shop.

Sometimes the whole world can seem like a misplayed note.
Sometimes colors fade and smear.

I sulk inside a nearby café,
where an old man plucks my sadness
on a tired requinto.

I remember another boy,
from long ago.
He used to sit alone and
write songs long into the night.

And when he became a man, he sang lullabies to his baby girl.
I'll never forget the bright colors emanating from their eyes. . . .
That is why I'm here.

I picture the boy from the shoe shop again.
La Música exists in the hearts of humans.
If I can't lead this child to his passion,
then what is my purpose?

I'm pulled out of my thoughts by the stray dog,
who's sniffing around the floor by my feet.
That's when it occurs to me: I don't have to do this alone.
I bend to whisper a new plan into Dante's ear.

The next morning is crisp and cloudless and smells of destiny.
As soon as Dante senses my presence, he tears the broom
out of the boy's hands and takes off.

He races through the alleys, into the plaza,
and up to the trash bin, where he barks
and howls and paws at the side.
"Dante!" the boy shouts, out of breath.
"What's wrong?"

And then he sees it.

During his shift at the shoe shop that night,
I wrap my arms around a pair of cackling cotorras
until the boy comes out to investigate.
The birds scurry, but not before the boy
has discovered the scattered nails.
He slips them into his pocket, sensing he's not alone.

Over the next several days, I track a light hammering
back up to the attic, where the boy is repairing the guitar.
When he finally gets it fixed he flips on the video
and maneuvers his fingers like the famous singer.

That weekend the boy sneaks his stringless guitar
past the shoe shop and heads for the plaza.
He sits on an empty bench beside Dante
and dreams of performing for a crowd.

It takes all my strength to summon a great gust of wind
that whips a músico's hat right off his head.
The man gives chase.
All through the crowded plaza they go.
Until he crashes into the boy.

El músico studies the familiar guitar.
He studies the boy.
Then he reaches into his bag
and hands over his last set of strings.
"Play what's in your heart," he says.
The boy nods and looks down at the strings.
All he can see is his family.

Before going to bed that night, he strings his repaired guitar
and tunes it and positions his fingers along the fretboard.
He glances down at Dante,
then looks up at his homemade ofrenda,
his heart thump thump thumping inside his chest.
He takes a deep breath and strums his fingers gently
across the nylon strings.

The boy doesn't know that in the ring of this first chord
he has become part of a grand harmony.
But here it is in the swirling skies above the attic.

And here it is in the wind whistling past
the windows of the shoe shop.

And here it is in the warm expression
on his mamá Coco's face.

One day these sounds may grow into songs
and color the hearts of others.
But for now he's just a boy in an attic with a guitar.
And the air he breathes is alive.